Have you read the other
Boyface books? . . .

BOYFACE AND tHE tARtAN BADGER

BOYFACE AND tHE UNCERtAIN PONIES

BOYFACE AND tHE POWER OF tHREE AND A BIt

AND THE QUANTUM CHROMATIC DISRUPTION MACHINE

WRITTEN BY

JAMES CAMPBELL

ILLUSTRATED BY

MARK WEIGHTON

Hodder Children's Books

For Nina, Joe, Hayden and Mrs Miggins with love, J.C.
For Seni, Eoin, Pops, Mills and Son with love, M.W.

HODDER CHILDREN'S BOOKS

First published in Great Britain in 2014 by Hodder and Stoughton

9 10

Text copyright© James Campbell, 2014
Illustrations copyright © Mark Weighton, 2014

The moral rights of the author and illustrator have been asserted.

A CIP catalogue record for this book
is available from the British Library.

ISBN 978 1 444 92207 3

Printed and bound in Great Britain
by Clays Ltd, St Ives plc

The paper and board used in this book
are made from wood from responsible sources.

Hodder Children's Books
An imprint of
Hachette Children's Group
Part of Hodder and Stoughton
Carmelite House
50 Victoria Embankment
London EC4Y 0DZ

An Hachette UK Company
www.hachette.co.uk

www.hachettechildrens.co.uk

Contents:

STRIPE ONE

SOME time about now, or maybe a little time ago. Or maybe more like halfway between a while ago and next Tuesday – yes, about then – there was a family. They were called the Antelope family. Now, you might think that a family with this name would be a family of antelopes, but you would be wrong. They were not antelopes at all. That was just their name.

You might perhaps wonder if they were called the Antelope family because they looked like antelopes. Well, you would be so wrong about this, that if you entered a competition to be right about things, you would be disqualified, thrown out, covered in buttercream and rolled in hundreds and thousands until you were sick. No, they didn't look like antelopes at all. Well, maybe they did a little bit.

But only in the same way that someone called Mrs Green might look a little bit green sometimes, or a man called Mr Butcher might look a bit like a sausage or a girl called Daisy might have a smile like the opening of a flower – and smell funny.

The Antelope family lived on the coast, next to beautiful shingly beaches, pebblish coves and sandy cliffs that towered over the waves like wavy towers. The sun shone almost every other day and many people had the unusual habit of strolling around normally, then suddenly bursting into giggles or explosive hiccups for no apparent reason. Between two of the sandiest cliffs was a pebblish cove where seagulls criss-crossed the sky, looking for chips to eat and new reasons to shout at each other. Pebbles sat in piles and blobs and heaps like heapy-blob-pile pebbles. Underwater, singing seadonkeys, waiting for their chance to shine, watched the village. The village of Stoddenage-on-Sea.

The Antelope family lived right in the

middle of this village in a complicated house that looked like it had been knocked together out of bits left over from other houses, in a fairly shoddy way, by someone who didn't know what they were doing. This was because the house had been built by Mrs Antelope, out of bits of other peoples' houses, in a really shoddy way. And she had no idea what she was doing.

Every time Mrs Antelope made a new friend and was invited round to their house for a cup of tea and a scone, she would steal a bit of the property (bricks, concrete, balconies or anything else she could break off), drag it back to the Antelope Family home and bodge it on with the wrong sort of glue and some tools she had lying around that weren't really meant for building with. This did, of course, cause something of a problem. The problem was that Mrs Antelope's new friend would very soon become her new ex-friend, and sometimes even become her enemy. The sort of enemy who would write angry letters saying, 'Dear Mrs Antelope,

where the flumming bling is my wall
and why did you steal it?' and 'Why
did you put part of my roof in your
pocket when you were round my
house having tea and a scone? Don't
say you didn't. You did. I saw you.'
And 'Why was my chimney up your
jumper and not on top of my house?
And why is it now on the top of your
house, you scandalous pooflip?'

Mrs Antelope was a large lady with
wrists as big as a tennis player's thigh.
She had a belly the size and shape of a
hot air balloon and when she laughed

her whole body would ripple and shudder and rumble and roar like an engine. Mrs Antelope was mad and lovely and everyone loved her madly. Until she stole something from them, of course. Then they weren't so sure.

Mrs Antelope's husband was called Mr Antelope. Mr Antelope looked very similar to his wife, but he had a hairier beard and his eyelashes were longer. The two of them were very much in love: they spent almost all of their time together, and scratched each other's itches in a happy kind of way. While Mrs Antelope was busy stealing bits of other people's houses, Mr Antelope was usually to be found in The Shop which was a cross between a factory, a workshop and a massive shed. They called it The Shop because they had always called it The Shop and it was in The Shop that Mr Antelope practised the ancient skill of Stripemongery.

Mr Antelope was a Stripemonger and had been a Stripemonger all his life. For many, many years he had mongered stripes: buying and selling stripes, adjusting stripes, collecting stripes, disposing of stripes and generally removing the stripes from one thing and sticking them to another.

Most of the business involved zebras. Mr and Mrs Antelope had been born in a faraway land called Tropical Antarctica. According to Mr Antelope's somewhat fanciful and probably untrue stories, Tropical Antarctica had far too many zebras. Apparently, there were loads out there: bumping into each other,

tripping over things, being tripped over by other things and generally getting in the way of everything.

When Mr and Mrs Antelope had moved to Stoddenage-on-Sea, they discovered that it was full of little girls and boys who wanted a pony to ride. And there just weren't enough ponies to go round.

Mr Antelope claimed that it was a simple case of supply and demand. Zebras were cheap in Tropical Antarctica and ponies were expensive in Stoddenage-on-Sea. He started importing massive amounts of the cheap zebras, removing their stripes and then selling them on as ponies to families who would love them, feed them carrots and sit on them.

The process of having their stripes removed was completely painless for the zebras. Sometimes it did tickle a bit, which made the zebras titter uncontrollably until they sneezed and sneezed and sneezed and then stopped abruptly as if nothing had happened.

To remove the stripes, Mr Antelope used The Quantum Chromatic Disruption Machine, which everyone just called The Machine.

'The Machine is quite simple, really,' Mr Antelope would explain to anyone who asked. 'It just alters the frequency vibrations on a quantum level, which are the smallest things that everything is made of. Like really tiny. Much tinier than anything you can see. Tinier than a mouse's bottom.' This would confuse most

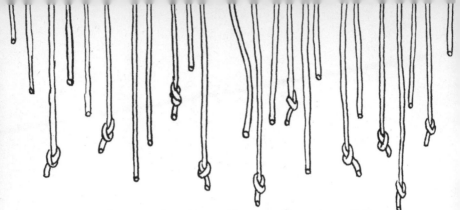

people and stop them from asking any more questions, but sometimes folks would want to know what that actually meant. 'Well, on a real life level,' Mr Antelope would wheeze, 'the zebras turn out looking like ponies.'

No one was ever really sure if Mr Antelope knew what he was talking about, or if he was just telling one of his fantastical stories. But they believed The Machine was pretty clever even if he wasn't. What was fantastically clever was that this process also produced a by-product: massive piles of black and white stripes.

These stripes were then kept in special boxes and sold to people who wanted to: jazz up a jumper by adding stripes; turn a sofa into something more exciting by adding stripes; make a car or skateboard go faster by adding stripes; or turn a pony into a zebra, by adding... er... stripes.

Mr Antelope also used The Machine to do the following things:

- Help leopards change their spots.

- Reduce tartan to a manageable level.

- Improve cats.

- Join up the dots on dalmatians to make rude pictures.

- Create compost out of homework.

- Repair guinea pigs.

The legends and the ancient books said that The Quantum Chromatic Disruption Machine could probably do more incredibly improbable things if operated properly by the right person. Theoretically, it could:

- Reproduce rainbows.

- Edit memories.

- Make afternoons go further.

- Slow people down until their thinking ticked like a clock.

⬭ Create black holes.

⬭ Change the weather.

⬭ Go sideways in time.

⬭ Produce maps of how things,
people and thoughts are
connected.

⬭ Help donkeys sing properly.

Mr and Mrs Antelope had one child, a
boy called Boyface. Boyface Antelope

was a boy like most boys but more so, and different.

Boyface Antelope was nine years, three hundred and sixty-four days old. And he looked it. Gangly ears, eyes like Christmas and more face than a cat. For the length of his life Boyface had not been allowed anywhere near the family Stripemongering business.

'You're too young,' his mum would say. 'You're not big enough!' his dad would growl.

'You're too stringy,' the seadonkeys would sing from under the water. 'Stringy and gangly. Thin as a seaweed. And weedy as a thingy.'

The seadonkeys would often sing strange songs. The people of Stoddenage-on-Sea would usually ignore them.

(AUTHOR'S NOTE: YOU MIGHT BE WONDERING WHAT ON EARTH THESE SEADONKEYS HAVE GOT TO DO WITH ANYTHING. TRUST ME, THEY WILL BECOME IMPORTANT LATER ON. NOT IN THIS BOOK BUT IN ONE OF THE

BOYFACE BOOKS THAT WILL FOLLOW.
PROBABLY NUMBER FOUR. MAYBE
NUMBER TWO. BUT MORE LIKELY
NUMBER FOUR.)

Boyface desperately wanted to learn about Stripemongering. He wanted to learn the secrets of The Quantum Chromatic Disruption Machine. He wanted to understand the ways of stripe removal and spot relocation. He longed to get a weasel and make its hair go all fluffy; fiddle with a flatfish; polish a frog; and even fulfil his dream to re-organise the hexagons on a giraffe. But his parents had told him that he wasn't allowed anywhere near The Shop until he was ten. That was the rule. His dad hadn't been allowed in the shop until he had turned ten. His dad's dad hadn't been allowed in until he had turned ten.

(AUTHOR'S NOTE: HIS DAD'S DAD'S DAD HAD DIED BEFORE THE AGE OF TEN.)

No one was allowed in The Shop until they were ten. That was the rule, they would tell him. Not until he was ten. In the meantime, he just loafed about, occasionally wandering into school by accident, listening to radio programmes about vegetable gardening, reading books about anything and generally wondering what everything was all about.

'Why can't I learn the business of Stripemongering?' Boyface would ask himself when he was curled up in bed. 'Why do I have to wait until I am ten? I'm only nine years, three hundred and sixty-four days old. Pooflips!'

STRIPE TWO

THE next day, however, something wonderful happened. It was his birthday and Boyface Antelope suddenly and unavoidably became ten years old. Shivering with excitement, Boyface skipped to his parents' room. Boyface loved going into his parents' bedroom because it was always warm and incredibly messy. It looked like an explosion in a charity shop. Piles of clothes (some dirty, some clean) were in every corner. Books and newspapers were arranged like walls, dividing the room into mini rooms full of saucepans, alarm clocks, boxes of stuff. Candlesticks. Tools. Engines. Brass objects. Pot plants. Piles of pictures in frames. And many, many rugs.

No one who ever saw Mr and Mrs Antelope's bedroom could help but wonder how on earth they ever found anything.

29

'It's easy,' Mr Antelope would explain with a grin. 'Everything is connected.' And everything was indeed connected; mainly by dusty cobwebs and spaghetti and string.

Boyface stepped through the doorway and looked quickly amongst the clutter for anything that looked like a tenth birthday present. Would he be given a new pair of trousers? Or maybe an empty goldfish bowl? Or even a duck that could quack the alphabet? He was very excited.

But as he looked at his parents, he realised that something was wrong, and that he probably wouldn't be getting any presents that day. Mr Antelope was lying on the bed. Mrs Antelope was mopping his forehead with a flannel and looking very worried. Mr Antelope looked even worse. He was green and puffy and ill. A massive bubble of shiny yellow nose glue had appeared from one of his nostrils and was growing bigger and bigger with each breath that he took. Boyface watched with fascination as it grew as big as his head and then finally burst, covering his dad's face with sticky yuckiness.

'Your dad is green and puffy and ill,' said Mrs Antelope.

'I'm green and puffy and ill,' confirmed Mr Antelope.

Boyface didn't know what to say. In all his ten years, he couldn't think of a single occasion when his dad had been ill. He just didn't get poorly. Surely he was too big to be sick.

Then, his parents hit him with the unexpected news. 'You will have to look after The Shop today,' croaked his dad.

Boyface was stunned. Him? Look after The Shop? He hadn't even been allowed to go in The Shop before, let alone look after it. Boyface was scared. 'Will I have to be sensible and responsible?' he asked.

'Yes, you will,' said Mr Antelope. 'Sensibly responsible and responsibly sensible.'

'Will Mum be able to help me?' asked Boyface.

'No,' said his mum. 'I'll be out stealing stuff.'

Mr Antelope used all of his strength to poke his wife in the ribs. He didn't really like it when she mentioned her stealing in front of Boyface. 'There is a manual though,' croaked Mr Antelope. 'It's only the first volume, but it should give you some of the basics and stop you from getting into too much trouble. It's on the side there, with the keys.'

Boyface stopped for a moment. 'But Dad,' he said. 'Can't we just close The Shop for a day? Or until you're better?'

Mr and Mrs Antelope exchanged glances, looked worried and sighed. 'The thing is,' said Mrs Antelope. 'It might take Dad more than a few days to get better. He might get worse first. Who knows?' As she said that she shrugged like a cross between a rug and a sheep.

Boyface did everything he could not

to cry, but a little bit did leak out. 'We need you to be sensibly responsible now, Boyface,' his mum said to him softly. 'Now that you're ten, it's time to begin your apprenticeship. It's time to learn the family business. One day, you might even have to be in charge.'

Boyface picked up the keys and the manual from his dad and walked out of his parents' bedroom, onto the landing, his bottom lip trembling.

'What am I going to do?' he asked himself with a squeak. 'I don't know anything about Stripemongering.'

As Boyface put the key into the lock of The Shop door he noticed how heavy the manual felt in his other hand. It was much bigger than any book he had ever held before. There would be plenty of advice in there, he was sure of it.

Slowly, Boyface opened the door that connected the house to The Shop. The door was a huge wooden one that Boyface's mum had nicked from a castle when she'd been helping out on a school trip. He remembered how she'd tried to squash it into his lunchbox when no one was looking. Boyface was only little at the time and had been really worried that he might get into trouble for stealing a door, but Mrs Antelope had said, 'If anyone says anything I'll tickle them on the nose with a bag of peas. Now be quiet and shove it up your jumper.' And that put his mind at ease. His mum was wonderful like that.

Now, a few years later, Boyface was opening that very same door into The Stripemongering Shop. The secret place that, until this morning, had been forbidden to him. He stepped through and into The Shop and had a look around. The castle doorway had led him into a place behind the counter. There was a mouldy office chair for his dad to sit on, and lots of packets of bubble wrap stacked on top of each other in tottering towers.

In one corner of The Shop were five orange plastic chairs that looked

like they had been stolen from a primary school. This was because Mrs Antelope had stolen them from Boyface's primary school during her one day as a teaching assistant.

These chairs were obviously some sort of reception area where customers would sit and ask his dad about stripes and spots and patterns and such.

The entrance from the street had always excited Boyface from the outside. It consisted of two doors, one inside the other. The big door stretched from the floor to the ceiling and allowed trucks and carts to get into the shop if they were delivering large loads of zebras or tartan or something. It was secured with huge iron bolts and complicated locks. It was so cumbersome to open and close that there was a smaller door inside the larger one that was just big enough for a person to step through, but not difficult to use. This door had a glass panel onto which a sign had been printed. Although it was backwards and fading, Boyface knew exactly what it said.

ANTELOPE AND CO.
STRIFEMONGERS,
DOT MANIPULATORS
AND COLOUR WIDENERS

STRICTLY NO CHILDREN
UNDER THE AGE OF TEN!

What particularly struck Boyface about The Shop was how disgustingly filthy everything was. It looked like it hadn't been cleaned for forty years. This was because it hadn't been cleaned for forty years.

There was all manner of complicated looking equipment, all over The Shop. Most of it meant nothing to Boyface, but some items were obvious. There was a huge pair of scales that looked like they could weigh a couple of zebras; a pile of bridles and saddles and riding bits that smelled of soap and horses; and everywhere were stacks of cardboard boxes – the weight of their contents misshaping their corners and sagging their edges.

Boyface felt a little bit scared and very much out of his depth. But he

remembered his dad had once said to him that it is only when we are out of our depth that we learn to swim.

He knew that he had to try to be sensibly responsible today, and so he sat down on the mouldy old chair and looked at the manual that his dad had given him.

Boyface opened up the book. The first page said just one thing:

DON'T TOUCH
THE QUANTUM CHROMATIC
DISRUPTION MACHINE.

Boyface suddenly realised that he had completely forgotten about The Quantum Chromatic Disruption Machine. He looked across The Shop to see The Machine entirely covered with seven or eight dirty brown sheets. Maybe they were to keep it clean. Maybe there were to keep it hidden. Maybe it was just somewhere to keep the dirty brown sheets.

Boyface ran over to The Machine, immediately deciding to ignore the words in the instruction manual. He couldn't leave it covered by sheets.

He had to see what it looked like. Until this day, he'd only ever seen The Machine from outside The Shop; through the grimy, dusty windows that hadn't been cleaned for forty years. Now, he was standing on the other side of those filthy panes of glass and holding the edge of the sheets. With a quick tug and a gasp, he pulled the sheets loose and they slid off The Machine, folding themselves up in a complex, crumpled heap on the floor. The Quantum Chromatic Disruption Machine was uncovered for Boyface to see.

The Machine was about the size of a small caravan. The sort of size of caravan in which you could fit two people for a short holiday. You could technically fit a couple more people, but after a while you'd have arguments about who had burnt the beans and why it was raining all the time. Eventually you would start wondering why you'd tried to get so many people into such a tiny caravan and then someone would get stuck in the loo and the fire service would have to come and unstick them with a bottle of olive oil and a really big

spoon. That was about the size of
The Quantum Chromatic Disruption
Machine.

The Quantum Chromatic Disruption
Machine was made from a collection
of different metals, rubber and
shiny plastic. It had tubes and pipes
coming out of one knobbly bit that
then connected into another knobbly
bit. There were flashing lights on the
top and on the side, with some in the
middle that seemed to be hiding so
you couldn't see them properly.

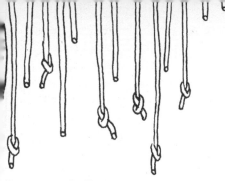

A filthy and ancient keyboard dangled off one corner. A conveyor belt was to be found at each end. One for taking things in. And one for spewing things out. There was a gigantic bucket for catching things; rubber strips over the entrances and exits; and dials and clockfaces that meant nothing to Boyface but said things like MIN and MAX and RUN! on them.

In places, it looked very badly taken care of, with scorch marks and dents and bits of tape covering cracks, but

at the same time it felt as though it was very much loved. It was difficult to describe but it was a bit like this:

Sometimes, when Boyface felt miserable, his mum would make pancakes. They weren't very good pancakes. They had burnt bits and lumpy bits and were usually quite ugly and tasted disgusting. But the way she made them involved a lot of effort, a lot of time, a lot of shouting and, most importantly, a lot of love. So even though the pancakes were gross, they made Boyface feel better when he ate them.

The Quantum Chromatic Disruption Machine had something of this pancake feel about it. Boyface was pleased about this, even though the last time he'd had his mum's pancakes he'd had such a poorly bottom that the downstairs toilet broke and half the village had to be evacuated.

(AUTHOR'S NOTE: A WHILE AGO, MRS ANTELOPE HAD TRIED TO TEACH BOYFACE HOW TO MAKE PANCAKES FOR HIMSELF. IT WENT QUITE WELL UNTIL THE TOSSING STAGE, WHEN BOYFACE GOT A PARTICULARLY HORRIBLE PANCAKE STUCK OVER HIS

FACE. MRS ANTELOPE HAD TRIED TO GET IT OFF BUT AFTER DECIDING IT WASN'T GOING TO BUDGE SHE SIMPLY POKED OUT SOME HOLES FOR HIS EYES AND NOSE AND SENT HIM OFF TO SCHOOL. MOST OF THE CHILDREN SAW THE FUNNY SIDE OF BOYFACE HAVING A PANCAKE FACE, BUT THREE TEACHERS FAINTED AND THE CARETAKER WAS SO FRIGHTENED HE WET HIMSELF.)

Boyface took a step backwards so he could see the whole machine in one go. It looked like a cross between an airport security x-ray machine and a car wash. Hanging off one of the exhaust pipes was a hand-written sign on a piece of cardboard that said:

UNAUTHORIZED PERSONS
KEEP OFF!

Boyface stood very still, gazing in awe at The Quantum Chromatic Disruption Machine. He could see the sign perfectly well and he knew that he wasn't allowed to touch it. But something inside him was trying to say otherwise. A deeper voice in his heart that felt older than him was suggesting that it wouldn't hurt to fire up The Machine, just to see what it looked like when it was running. He wouldn't have to try and do anything complicated. Just switch it on.

His thoughts and feelings were interrupted, however, by a knock at the door to the street. Boyface froze. Who could that be?

STRIPE THREE

Boyface unlocked the smaller door to the street and stood back. 'Come in please, I think,' he said as boldly as he could. The door opened slowly, triggering a bell mechanism, and a mixture of tinkling and sunshine filled The Shop, glanced off the dust and danced through the rust and dirt.

When the sound of the bell stopped and Boyface had got used to the sunlight, he stood, his mouth open wide like a stuck fish, as a little girl stepped into The Shop. Boyface immediately recognised her from school. On the occasional day when he accidentally found himself in Stoddenage-on-Sea Primary, he was in the same class as this little girl. Her name was Clootie Whanger.

Clootie Whanger was a medium-sized little girl with auburn hair in plaits, a freckled face and probably the loudest voice ever fitted to a child of her size. Clootie had always been loud. When she was a baby, Stoddenage-on-Sea had held a competition to see who was the loudest in the village. It had to be abandoned, however, because no one could hear the competitors over the noise of baby Clootie's crying and bawling.

'Hello Clootie,' said Boyface. 'What are you doing here?'
'It's my birthday,' shouted Clootie proudly. 'I'm ten today.'
'That's a coincidence,' said Boyface

with a raise of his eyebrows. 'I'm ten today, too.'

'Oh, pooflips!' shouted Clootie sadly. 'I thought it was just me.'

And so, Clootie and Boyface realised something – they had the same birthday! Boyface had never met anyone with the same birthday as him and neither had Clootie, so for a moment they were a bit confused.

'Are you sure it's your birthday today?' asked Boyface with a giggle.

'Yes I am,' shouted Clootie seriously.

'I've brought proof.' Boyface was
slightly deaf from all the shouting
but he looked carefully at the
massive red badge that was pinned
to Clootie's lapel.

It had
TEN TODAY
printed on it.

'Gosh,' said Boyface. 'I haven't got one of those... But why have you come here to my parents' Stripemongering Shop?'

Clootie loudly explained that, for as long as she could remember, she had walked past The Shop on her way home from school and had longed to come inside. Something had been drawing her in. She had put her ear against the walls and tried to peer through the dirty windows as the rumbling and throbbing noises of The Quantum Chromatic Disruption

Machine rolled into the street. 'What magic is taking place in that shop?' she had said to herself. 'What was that machine doing?' she had asked her Mum. 'When can I go in there and see for myself?' she had asked the sign on the front door, which replied, of course, with:

STRICTLY NO CHILDREN UNDER THE AGE OF TEN.

And so, for years, Clootie had waited for this day. This special day when she could use her 'Ten Today' badge as proof of age, enter The Stripemongers Shop and meet Mr Antelope for the very first time.

'Wow,' said Boyface. 'It's a shame my Dad is green and puffy and ill then, isn't it?'

Boyface explained how he had been put in charge for the day and Clootie was indeed a little bit disappointed about this, so Boyface asked her if she'd like to spend the day with him anyway and help him explore

The Shop together. Clootie was very excited about this. The two of them started by looking for something interesting to play with.

The most interesting thing in The Shop was, of course, The Machine. Boyface and Clootie stood in front of it, staring at how startlingly beautiful it was. They tried to follow its tubes and pipes to see where they connected, but it was just too complicated.

'Where did it come from?' asked Clootie.

Boyface sat down with Clootie Whanger and told her the story of how his parents had come to Stoddenage-on-Sea in the olden days. Well, as much as he knew, anyway. The story of The Quantum Chromatic Disruption Machine, you see, was something that Mr and Mrs Antelope had always told him at bed time. The only problem with this was that Boyface would always fall asleep before the end of the story, and in the morning he could never remember exactly what the story was and which bit went where and which bits were true and which bits were from his dreams.

'It came from Tropical Antarctica,' Boyface began. 'I've never been there and it sounds a bit made-up to me, but Dad says it's real and that it's where we get the zebras from. Mum says it's somewhere between the Arctic and Antarctica and I don't know what she means by that. Before I was born, when Mum and Dad were young, The Machine was owned by my granddad.'

Boyface then told the tale of how one day, a great number of years ago, Granddad Antelope gave The Machine to Mr Antelope and his new wife and told them to travel to a new and magical village called Stoddenage-on-Sea where they would find their fame and fortune. Neither of them knew why Granddad Antelope had done this, but Mrs Antelope reckoned he was trying to get rid of them.

The young Mr and Mrs Antelope sailed from Tropical Antarctica by boat and, after months on the towering waves, they and The Machine arrived on the shinglish beach in the pebblish cove of Stoddenage-on-Sea. They wandered around the village with only The Machine and the clothes they had on. Very poor, but rich in love. They were so poor, in fact, that they had to share underwear.

'That's disgusting,' said Clootie loudly.

'They still do,' explained Boyface. 'It's

okay, though, because their bottoms are exactly the same size (and shape).'

'That's still disgusting,' shouted Clootie. 'Why didn't they get jobs so they could afford to buy more underwear?'

'They didn't need to get jobs,' smiled Boyface. 'They had The Quantum Chromatic Disruption Machine. And they used to it to monger stripes and sell stuff.'

Mrs Antelope gently and lovingly stole a wheelbarrow and, between the two of them, they got The Machine on top of it.

Mrs Antelope would wheel the thing through the streets, waddling and wobbling. Mr Antelope would march out in front, calling out as loud as he could, 'Any old stripes! Any old stripes! Polka dots you don't want any more! Badgers you've had enough of! Get them out here. We'll have them! Any old stripes! Cats you don't like! Any old stripes! Top prices paid. Any old stripes!'

OFF

IN

OBSERVATION

ON

DO NOT TOUCH

An old lady might pop out of her house in her slippers and cardigan with a stripy ferret. 'How much will you give me for this?' she'd screech enchantingly.

'Well, we'll see, won't we?' Mr Antelope would purr. He would hold the ferret up to the light, measure its weight with his hands and then give it to his wife for her opinion. While she stretched it and sniffed it, Mr Antelope's voice would melt into a delicious and treacly storytelling style of talking in a fantastical kind of way.

'I do like your slippers, old lady.'

'Why, thank you.'

'But don't you think they are a bit plain?'

'Do you really think so?'

'Yes, I do. What they need, gorgeous lady, is to be TARTAN!'

(AUTHOR'S NOTE: MR ANTELOPE HAD A HABIT OF CALLING ALL LADIES GORGEOUS EVEN WHEN THEY WERE CLEARLY ANCIENT AND HAD FACES SO WRINKLY THAT YOU COULD PLAY THEM LIKE XYLOPHONES.)

'Tartan?'

'Tartan. All the best old ladies in Stoddenage-on-Sea are wearing tartan slippers these days. I'll tell you what, we'll use The Machine here to tartanise your slippers.'

'Tartanise my slippers?'

'Exactly. That's what this marvellous machine can do for you.'

'But how much will that cost?'

Mr Antelope would get out a notepad and a tiny stub of a pencil – which he would wet with the end of his tongue – then write out some calculations.

'It'll only cost you the following,' he would pronounce. 'One cardigan; one ferret; two cups of tea; all the money in the jar by your front door; a good book; a packet of felt-tip pens and a fried egg sandwich, not too runny.'

'That sounds like a brilliant deal,' the old lady would say, handing Mr Antelope her slippers. 'Tartanise me up, Mr Antelope.'

And that was how the Antelopes earned their living in the early days.

For the first year of living in Stoddenage-On-Sea, Mr and Mrs Antelope were homeless. They slept on a derelict piece of land which they had found in the middle of the village. People said that it used to be an aquarium, but that it had burned down in a fire many years before. Now it was just a patch of land, covered in thistles and rubble, nettles and charred fish.

Each night, they would hide The Quantum Chromatic Disruption Machine behind some of the taller thistles and snuggle up together to keep warm. One night Mr Antelope said to his wife, 'Do you know what I'd like for a present, my darling?'

'What's that?' Mrs Antelope replied through a mouthful of fried egg sandwich.

'A wall. A nice strong wall to lean on when I'm thinking.'

So that night, while her husband was asleep, Mrs Antelope crept through the village and stole a wall from the side of the flower shop.

The next morning, Mr Antelope was so pleased that he asked for something else.

'Do you know what I'd like for a present, my darling?'

'What's that?' Mrs Antelope replied through a mouthful of stripy ferret. 'Some more walls and a roof and stuff.'

'And that,' explained Boyface to Clootie, his new wide-eyed friend, 'is how the house and The Shop got built.'

'One night, however, my mum said to my dad, "Do you know what I'd like for a present, my darling?"
"What's that?" Dad asked through a mouthful of cardigan.
"A baby," said my mum. And that's how I came along.'

'That was a lovely story,' said Clootie quietly, and as Boyface looked at her to say thank you, he noticed that she was looking a bit sad. And wasn't shouting.

'You're looking a bit sad,' said Boyface, surprised. 'That's strange. It's not a sad story.'

'I know,' said Clootie. 'I'm not sad. I just get a bit tearful sometimes when people tell me happy things.'

Boyface wasn't sure what to make of this. 'Let me give you a hug,' he said. But as he leant forward, Clootie pulled away.

'No thank you,' she shouted. 'I don't need a hug.'

Boyface thought this was very strange; in his family, if anyone felt sad or happy or any sort of feeling, really, they always got a hug. Maybe things were different in Clootie's house. He was about to ask her about this when there was a loud knocking at the door to the street.

'Oh. Who is there, please?' he asked. 'And what do you want?'

Huffing and puffing like a steam train falling over, whoever had knocked at the door shouted, 'Delivery for Antelope here! And it's very, very heavy!!!'

85

BOYFACE opened the door as quickly as he could. Eventually, in tottered Mr Pointless with a massive suitcase held precariously on his shoulders.

'Hello Boyface,' he groaned. 'Are you in charge today then?'

'Um... I think so,' said Boyface. 'Dad is green and puffy and ill and in bed, and it's my tenth birthday today so I have to be sensibly responsible.'

Boyface had met Mr Pointless many times in the café on Sundays. He was a delivery man. He had a big, grumbly old van and muscled shoulders that rippled and popped like bubble wrap as he lifted and carried wardrobes and boxes, sofas and grandfather clocks, pianos and parcels, large and heavy.

'Talking of large and heavy,' grunted Mr Pointless. 'Where do you want this?'

Boyface wasn't sure so he nodded at a space on the floor and shrugged with his eyebrows.

Mr Pointless lowered the massive suitcase to the floor with a thud that

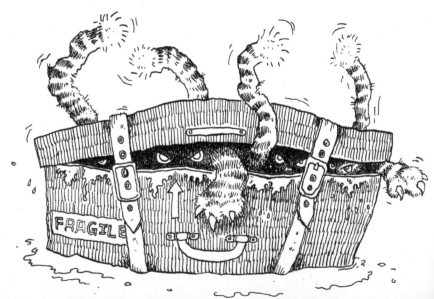

caused a minor explosion of dust to shoot up into the air and hover in a filthy cloud like a visible fart. This made Clootie cough.

'Oh, hello there,' said Mr Pointless. 'You're that ... um ... so-and-so's little ... the one with the shouty voice.'

'I'm Clootie Whanger,' shouted Clootie Whanger, louder than ever. 'I haven't got a shouty voice and I am ten today as well. Look at my badge!'

'Ten today?' exclaimed a puffed-out Mr Pointless, wiping the sweat off his face, a face splattered with oil like a garage floor. 'How time flies. I can remember you both when you were tiny babies with no teeth, sitting in the corner of the pub eating crisps and drinking beer. Sign here.'

Boyface couldn't remember being a tiny baby and he didn't understand what was meant by 'sign here', but Mr Pointless waved a piece of paper in front of his nose which detailed the delivery. He wanted Boyface to sign his name to say that he had received the suitcase and was now responsible for it. Boyface had never done anything like that before. He'd never been responsible for anything, really, so he read the piece of paper very carefully.

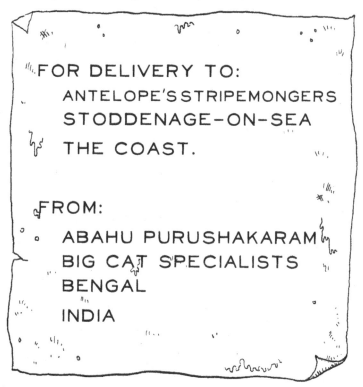

FOR DELIVERY TO:
    ANTELOPE'S STRIPEMONGERS
    STODDENAGE–ON–SEA
    THE COAST.

FROM:
    ABAHU PURUSHAKARAM
    BIG CAT SPECIALISTS
    BENGAL
    INDIA

Boyface signed his name underneath the address. Clootie looked very impressed at how sensibly responsible he was being. And he felt a little bit proud of himself, until he noticed what was printed below his signature.

DELIVERY OF:
ONE BIG SUITCASE
CONTAINING
FIVE IRRITABLE TIGERS

Boyface read that last bit out loud. 'Five Irritable Tigers.' He looked at

Mr Pointless in horror, then he looked at the massive, bulging suitcase in even more horror.

'What am I supposed to do with five irritable tigers?' he cried.

'I dunno,' shrugged Mr Pointless. 'But what your dad normally does is sticks 'em through The Quantum Chromatic Disruption Machine, removes their stripes and then mucks about with them. Why don't you try that?' And with that, Mr Pointless gave Boyface a cheeky smile, Clootie a pat on the head and set off towards the door, whistling as he went.

'Wait,' shouted Boyface. 'You can't just leave us with a suitcase full of irritable tigers. I've never done any Stripemongering before. Can you give me some advice?'

Mr Pointless stopped and turned round quickly. 'Well,' he began with a stroke of his dirty chin. 'I don't know anything about Stripemongering, but I have found with many things that you should always be true to your heart.'

'And what does that mean?' asked Boyface.

Mr Pointless looked at the ceiling and then back at the two children. 'You'll work it out,' he chuckled and then skipped through the door like a wallaby.

Boyface and Clootie watched Mr Pointless leave and then turned their attention to the suitcase, particularly to the zips and the buckles and the bulges and the bumps. Could there really be five tigers squashed in there?

'Why do you think they're so irritable?' shouted Clootie nervously.

'Probably because they've been squashed into a suitcase,' mused Boyface. 'That would make me irritable.'

Suddenly, one of the bulges changed shape and moved slightly. Boyface stopped breathing. Clootie hid her face.

'I think they're awake,' whispered Boyface. 'What are we going to do?'

Boyface truly had no idea what to do. He had no idea how to be a Stripemonger. He had no idea how The Quantum Chromatic Disruption Machine worked. He had no idea how to remove the stripes from tigers. He had no idea how to muck about with them either. He had no idea if the tigers would be dangerous but he was guessing they would be. How do you unpack five irritable tigers safely? If he unpacked them wrongly or put them through The Machine in an inappropriate way they might get more than irritable. They might get furious.

But he couldn't just leave them squashed in a suitcase in the middle of The Shop floor all day. What if someone tripped over them? Maybe he should ask his dad. Yes that was it. He would go upstairs and say, 'I'm very sorry to wake you, Dad. I'm sorry that you're poorly but there's a massive suitcase of irritable tigers in The Shop and I don't know what to do with them.'

'You can't do that,' bellowed Clootie with a gasp. 'You're supposed to be sensibly responsible today.'

'You're right,' said Boyface defiantly. 'I might as well go into their bedroom and say, "Dad, I'm not good enough for this. I can't be responsible for The Shop. I'm no use to you. I'm not big enough. I'm not a Stripemonger. I'm not an Antelope. Your journey here from overseas was a waste of time. I'm a failure".'

'But you're not a failure, Boyface. You are a Stripemonger!' yelled Clootie. 'Your name is Boyface Antelope and you are a Stripemonger! Your dad is a Stripemonger. Your dad's dad was

a Stripemonger. I know you can do it. You're only a failure if you don't even try.'

'Right then,' said Boyface with that new strong voice he had found deep inside him. 'Let's stop mucking about and monger some stripes.'

The two of them paced over to the suitcase. It was properly moving now and from all the rocking and wobbling it looked like the

tigers had woken up. As if to confirm this, a growl came from inside, followed by a muffled roar.

'Right,' said Boyface. 'I'm going to unpack the tigers. But first, I'm going to switch on The Quantum Chromatic Disruption Machine!'

'What are you thinking?' screamed Clootie, suddenly changing her mind about the whole thing. 'You'll get into terrible trouble.'

'I don't care,' said Boyface. 'Maybe The Machine will scare the tigers or something. It doesn't matter. Something will happen. I'm listening to my heart! Listening to the voice inside myself.'

Another muffled roar came from inside the suitcase and it tipped sideways and span around. The tigers in it were clearly very irritable indeed. To make things even worse, Clootie could hear the sound of the tigers clawing and biting at the zip of the suitcase. They were definitely trying to find a way out.

'Maybe we should read the instructions first!' shouted Clootie. But Boyface was determined. He grabbed hold of the ON/OFF switch, took a deep breath and...

'Boyface! Stop what you are doing immediately!'

The words came from the doorway leading into into the house and they came from two voices. Two people at once. Mr Antelope and Mrs Antelope. Boyface's mum and his dad.

Boyface froze like a lollipop with his hand still holding the switch. Then he slowly turned around, expecting to be in terrible trouble. But straight away he saw that his mum and dad weren't cross at all. They were

smiling and laughing, their massive
bellies shuddering and bouncing like
lawnmowers.

'Hello Mum. Hello Dad,' he said
through his teeth. 'I wasn't going to
switch it on.'
'Yes you were, you wonderful lump
of boy-shaped cake-mix,' his dad
boomed with pride. 'Now come over
here and give us a hug.'

As Boyface let himself be gently
suffocated by the fleshy folds of his dad
and lovingly bruised by the muscles

of his mum, he suddenly realised that his dad wasn't green and puffy and ill any more. He pulled himself out of the hug and said, 'Hang on a minute. How come you're not green and puffy and ill any more? And how come I'm not in loads of trouble?'

Mr Antelope ruffled his son's hair and the three of them sat down on the stolen school chairs so that Mr and Mrs Antelope could explain what the flipping poo was going on.

STRIPE FIVE

IT turned out that the whole thing had been a test to see if Boyface could be trusted to help with the family business. A test to see if he would be sensibly responsible. A test to find out if he was a true Stripemonger. A normal ten year old, you see, would have listened to the instructions and not gone anywhere near The Quantum Chromatic Disruption Machine. A Stripemonger, however, will always switch The Machine on, no matter how stupid or dangerous that might be.

(AUTHOR'S NOTE: NOT WORRYING TOO MUCH ABOUT WHETHER THINGS ARE STUPID AND DANGEROUS OR NOT IS POSSIBLY WHY THERE AREN'T MANY STRIPEMONGERS LEFT IN THE WORLD.)

Boyface had shown that there was something different in his heart.

'Obviously, we had to stop you before you did anything,' explained Mr Antelope. 'Until I've taught you how to work The Machine safely, you might accidentally create a black hole and suck the universe up its own bottom.'

'So you weren't really ill?' Boyface said, still a little confused.

'Of course, he wasn't,' laughed Mrs Antelope. 'Look at the size of him! He's too big to get ill.'

'From now on,' said Mr Antelope beaming with pride. 'You are officially a Stripemonger. An apprentice for the moment and probably an apprentice for the next ten years or so. But over those ten years I shall teach you the ways of the Stripemonger and how to work The Quantum Chromatic Disruption Machine. Just like my old dad taught me.'

Boyface was so pleased with himself. He wasn't quite sure why his dad had pretended to be ill, and he had no idea how Mr Antelope had produced

snot bubbles from a perfectly healthy nose, but he had long since decided that he didn't need to understand anything in order to be happy.

'So, did you know that five irritable tigers were going to be delivered?' he asked his dad.

'I ordered them specially,' laughed Mr Antelope.

'But what on earth are we going to do with them?' Boyface asked.

'I'll show you,' said Mr Antelope with a grin.

Mr Antelope spent the rest of the day showing Boyface the basics of setting up The Machine. When it was switched on, it made the most amazing sounds: crunching and whirring and an occasional weird glooping sound that made Boyface think it was eating itself.

Once The Machine was warm, they set about the delicate operation of unpacking the tigers. Mr Antelope

carefully opened the suitcase to reveal five very squashed, and very irritable, man-eating giant cats.

Before the tigers had a chance to do any damage, Mrs Antelope flicked them all on the nose with a bag of peas. This didn't stop them from being irritable, but at least they were quiet for a while.

Mr Antelope and his son loaded the stunned tigers into The Machine and, with more whirring and gloopy swallowing noises, they removed the tigers' stripes.

'What shall we do with them?' asked Boyface excitedly.

'Well,' said his dad with a smirk, 'let's muck about with them.'

And muck about with them they did. First they discovered that a tiger with no stripes is beige. Then they tried putting zebra stripes on one of the tigers and the thick stripes looked brilliant.

'I'll get a fortune for that down the market!' said Mr Antelope.

Next, they tried sorting out all the colours. They made one red tiger, one orange tiger, one yellow tiger and one black tiger. They looked really weird.

At one point, Boyface pressed the wrong button and one of the tigers imploded and turned into a bowl of stripy pasta. Whoops.

'Wow,' said Boyface. 'I wasn't expecting that. Will it be okay?'

'Of course it'll be okay,' giggled Mr Antelope. 'We can fix it with this

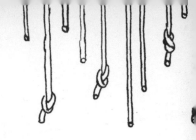

special button that turns it back into a tiger. It doesn't matter if you make mistakes.'

And he was right. It didn't matter. What did matter was that Boyface was learning something from his dad. He had never seen his dad work before, had never seen how quickly sausagey fingers could work the controls. Until that day, his dad had been someone who fell asleep in his chair. Now, Boyface could see that he was a genius Stripemonger. Until that day, work had been

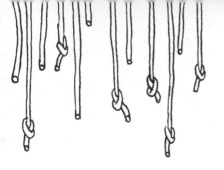

something Mr Antelope had carried out away from his son. Something that had kept them apart. For the last ten years, Stripemongering was something Boyface wasn't allowed to do. Not allowed to be a part of. Today, however, he'd been given the key to the door. He'd been allowed inside and he had proved himself. He was only an apprentice Stripemonger and he still had a lot to learn. But he had made a start and there would be many, many more Stripemongering adventures ahead of him.

At around three o'clock, Clootie had to go home. She'd had an amazing day watching The Machine at work. 'This is the best day I've ever had, Boyface,' she shouted quietly. 'But I have to go home now or I'll be in terrible trouble.'

Boyface was so pleased to have made friends with Clootie. He wanted to give her a hug, but remembered that she didn't do hugs. So he held his hand out for a handshake. Clootie paused for a moment like she didn't know what to do. Then she took his hand in hers, lifted it gently up to her face and blew a raspberry on his knuckles.

'Thank you for having me!' shouted Clootie Whanger as she skipped off home.

At the end of that day, Boyface and his mum and dad tidied up the shop, put the remaining tigers in a cupboard and switched off The Quantum Chromatic Disruption Machine.

Boyface helped put the sheets back on top of it, then the Antelopes went through to the house and into the kitchen to eat his mum's disgusting pancakes. After they had all been to the toilet, Mr Antelope took his son up the spiral stairs to the roof for a little chat.

The two of them sat contentedly on a bit of roof that Mrs Antelope had stolen from the police station when she'd been visiting there once. They sat there in silence for a while, smiling happily as they looked out across the village and the sea. The sea was calm and the moon looked down on them like a snooty cheese. Out in the water, the seadonkeys watched them from under huge cargo ships, planning things. But that's for a different story.

'So now you're ten,' said Mr Antelope carefully, 'I think we should talk about your own stripes. I've got a present for you.'

Boyface's dad pulled an envelope from his pocket. It was crumpled and had a coffee stain on it, so Boyface could tell that it was very special. 'Can I open it?' asked Boyface quietly.

'Of course,' said his dad with a whisper. Boyface opened the envelope. Inside was a set of stripes like you'd get in the army but they were rainbow coloured and shone like gold, as if they had been woven out of some sort of magical thread. As Boyface turned them over in his hands they caught the moonlight so beautifully that he nearly cried. Not because he was sad. It was a different sort of feeling and it was new to him.

'You are holding the stripes of a Stripemonger,' said Mr Antelope.

'You can sew them on your shirt tomorrow.'

That night, Boyface was curled up in bed with a hot water bottle and a torch. He was very pleased. 'I did well today, didn't I?' he giggled to himself. 'I don't think I'll have another tenth birthday like it.'

Then he switched off his torch, went straight to sleep and dreamed his day all over again.

THE END